For the Pippins
—D. C.

For Caitlyn Dlouhy and Ann Bobco
—B. L.

ATHENEUM BOOKS FOR YOUNG READERS
An imprint of Simon & Schuster Children's Publishing Division
1230 Avenue of the Americas, New York, New York 10020
Text copyright © 2018 by Doreen Cronin
Illustrations copyright © 2018 by Betsy Lewin
ATHENEUM BOOKS FOR YOUNG READERS is a registered trademark of Simon & Schuster, Inc.
Atheneum logo is a trademark of Simon & Schuster, Inc.
For information about special discounts for bulk purchases, please contact Simon & Schuster Special Sales at
1-866-506-1949 or business@simonandschuster.com.
The Simon & Schuster Speakers Bureau can bring authors to your live event. For more information or to book an event,
contact the Simon & Schuster Speakers Bureau at 1-866-248-3049 or visit our website at www.simonspeakers.com.
Book design by Ann Bobco
The text for this book was set in Filosofia.
The illustrations for this book were rendered in watercolor.
Manufactured in China
0418 SCP
First Edition
2 4 6 8 10 9 7 5 3 1
CIP data for this book is available from the Library of Congress.
ISBN 978-1-5344-1449-5
ISBN 978-1-5344-1450-1 (eBook)

Click, Clack, QUACK to School!

Doreen Cronin · *Illustrated by* **Betsy Lewin**

A CAITLYN DLOUHY BOOK
Atheneum Books for Young Readers
New York London Toronto Sydney New Delhi

On Monday, Duck brought a letter to Farmer Brown.
Some of it was written in crayon:

Dear Farmer Brown,

Please be our guest at our Farm Day
Lunch tomorrow.
Bring the animals, too!
Love,
Dinkelmeyer Elementary School

PS   What is your favorite color?
PPS How old are you?
PPPS We have a turtle.

Farmer Brown was so excited. He had not been
to school in a very, very, very long time!

He must get the animals ready.

"We are going to school tomorrow!"
he told the cows. "We must get ready!"

The cows had never been to school.
They were so excited!

They stomped and clomped and
MOO, MOO, MOOed!

"School is very quiet," said Farmer Brown. "There is no clomping; no stomping; and no

moo, MOO, MOOing."

The cows were not so excited anymore.

"We are going to school tomorrow!"
Farmer Brown told the chickens.

The chickens had never been to school.
They were so excited!

They clapped and snapped and
cluck, cluck, clucked!

"School is very serious," said Farmer Brown.
"There is no clapping; no snapping;
and no
cluck, cluck, clucking."

The chickens were not so excited anymore.

Farmer Brown arrived at the pigpen.
"We are going to school tomorrow!" he announced.

The pigs had never been to school.
They were so excited!

They hooted and hollered and **oink, oink, oink**ed!

"School is very calm," said Farmer Brown. "There is no hooting; no hollering; and no oink, oink, oinking."

The pigs were not so excited anymore.

Farmer Brown arrived at the barn.
Duck was meditating.

"We are going to school tomorrow!" said Farmer Brown.
"And there will be no stomping, clomping, snapping,
clapping, hooting, or hollering."

Duck breathed in **slowly and deeply**.

"And try not to be so Duck-y,"
said Farmer Brown.

Duck breathed out **slowly and deeply**.

Farmer Brown handed out rule books,
and the animals studied all night.

No stomping.
No clomping.
No moo, moo, mooing.

No clapping.
No snapping.
No cluck, cluck, clucking.

No hooting.
No hollering.
No oink, oink, oinking.

Don't be Duck-y.

The next morning, they lined up quietly
in front of the truck with no stomping, clomping,
clapping, snapping, hooting, or hollering.

Farmer Brown was so proud!

They were quiet and still on the ride to school.
The cows were not mooey.
The chickens were not clucky.
The pigs were not oinky.

Duck breathed in **s l o w l y   a n d   d e e p l y**.
Duck breathed out **s l o w l y   a n d   d e e p l y**.

Farmer Brown was so proud!

When they arrived, they got off the truck quietly
and waited in the empty school yard.

The school seemed quiet, serious, and calm.

And then the bell rang for recess.

The doors flew open, and the yard
was suddenly filled with . . .

wiggling and *giggling,*

thunking
and
clunking,

chirping and chattering,

squeaking and
squealing, and

zooming and zigging.

So the cows got mooey and
stomp, clomp, stomped!

And the chickens got clucky and
clap, snap, clapped!

And the pigs got oinky and
holler, hoot, hollered!

And the mice read graphic novels in the shade.

Inside the school,
Duck was just Duck-y.

Dear FARMER BROWN

Thank You For VISITING

OUR SCHOOL

Bobby